Bigfoot Sasquatch Files

Volume 6

By Kevin E. Lake

These stories are true.

Potentially...

1

Winds Of November

The scariest night we ever spent in our house (so far) was the first. It's been four years ago now, and I'll never forget it. We'd finally gotten everything we'd been wanting for the longest time and we had no idea just how frightening that would be.

Silence.

Total.

We'd only recently moved to the U.S., central Virginia to be exact, from the Philippine Islands, where we'd spent our last six months in the capital city of Manila, close to the U.S. embassy, so that the second my now wife's fiance visa was granted we could jump on the next plane to the U.S., which we did. While there, we lived in a nice condo on the thirty third floor of a seventy story high skyscraper right in the middle of the city. And despite the height, all we heard, all day and all night, was the honking of horns, the screeching of brakes and tires, and the shouts and screams of people. All we saw were lights, lights, and more lights at night, and smog, smog and more smog by day. It made us long for a place out in the middle of nowhere, where there were no people, and where there was no smog, and where there were no noises other than the noises of nature. After having made it to the U.S., and spending a few months in an apartment complex nearly as rambunctious as Manila, we finally found our little homestead out in the middle of nowhere, we bought it, and the dream had been achieved.

And that first night, again, was absolutely terrifying!

I grew up in the mountains of Appalachiastan, and all I'd ever known for the first quarter century of my life was silence at night, and mostly by day, once you got off the well beaten path, that is. But that was years ago. I left Appalachiastan and I spent time in places like Seattle, and then on to Iraq (yes, a war zone), and then the Philippines. Somehow, and though it drove me crazy at first, I'd gotten used to the noises of the city, the combat zone, and both the rural and urban jungles of Southeast Asia. I'd forgotten the peace and tranquility of those beautiful country nights, though after years away from them, I longed for them, and yet when I got them back? Well, we've discussed this. No need to be redundant. I know, too late.

I remember that first night, lying in bed. It was a brand new king size that we'd had custom made for our new home. Well, new to us. It's nearly one hundred and twenty years old, one of the last sharecropper houses built in the U.S., just before the industrial revolution would come along and change the landscape of the world economy, and with it, the world's way of living. My wife was on the opposite side of the bed that night, and our son, only five years old at the time, was sleeping in between us.

Neither my wife nor my son had any problem falling asleep that first night. Not only had we spent the entire weekend moving our belongings from our apartment twenty miles away in the city (it took a few trips and two days of work), but our son had started kindergarten just a couple of weeks before. It was September. And we'd just gone through the jumping through hoops bullshit with his school in order for them to allow him to attend.

You see, when we had our apartment in the city, we were in one of the overcrowded, understaffed city school districts. But where our house is located, we are in the most privileged school district in the county. Many of the kids who attend this school come from the families of trust babies and celebrities, and the school, though public, is better than most expensive private schools in the U.S. It's a huge part of the reason we bought our house where we did.

We finally stood on one leg long enough, while rubbing our bellies with one hand and patting our heads with the other, after having given the principal a notarized copy of our real estate contract, showing we were closing on our house, in his school district, only two weeks after the beginning of the school year, and permission for our son to attend the school was finally granted. It was an emotionally exhaustive process to go through while also going through the emotional process of buying a house, all while going through the physically draining process of moving from our apartment to our house only three months after having moved nine thousand miles away from the Philippines to Virginia.

Ugh!

But despite this, and being plenty exhausted myself, I could not sleep.

It was too quiet.

Far too quiet.

And my mind began playing tricks on me.

In Mosul, Iraq, where I was stationed, our team ran night missions, and we tried to sleep during the day. *Tried* being the key word here. It was difficult, as our base, Diamondback it was called, was right in the center of the city, and our enemies who lived in the city would lob mortars at us all day, trying to kill us while we tried to sleep in their attempts to keep us from coming out at night. Just like the diamondback rattlesnakes that we were. Eventually, by about halfway through the deployment, we were all on trazadone, which I equate to a horse tranquilizer, because trust me, once you take it, you are knocked the fuck out for the next eight hours. It allowed us to sleep through the barrage of mortars that never stopped the entire time we were there.

And you might think that sleep in the middle of the jungle in the most remote locations of the Philippines, after that, would be easier, but it was actually harder. You see, Filipinos love to sing, especially when they're drunk, and there are these little karaoke bars all over the islands. And by bars, I mean just these little bamboo shacks where the proprietor is one of the few in the village fortunate enough to be able to afford electricity, allowing them to purchase or lease a karaoke machine that the locals pay one pesos (about two cents in U.S. money) to sing a karaoke song. And they do this until 3:00 a.m., with the volume on high, and the entire village gets to hear it all. And then, at 5:00 a.m., the morning vendors start roaming through the villages, screaming at the top of their lungs, what it is they're selling.

"Isda! Isda!" the fish vendors yell.

"Gulai! Gulai!" the vegetable vendors yell.

And sleep, at least for westerners not accustomed to such behavior, becomes as elusive as, well, for the lack of a better comparison…

…Bigfoot Sasquatch.

But as I lay in that brand new, overpriced custom made king size bed that first night in our new house on our Virginia homestead, my mind got the better of me and it kept me from sleep. At least in Iraq, when I heard the mortars, I knew who or what was out there. A bunch of people trying to kill me. When I was in the Philippines, as loud as it was out in the jungles at night, I knew what was out there. Drunken Filipinos crucifying Bon Jovi and Journey. Little old men with slimy eats from the sea and their little old wives selling the products of their labor in their gardens. And even in Manilla I'd learned to differentiate the sound of a taxi cab's horn and that of a jeepney. But here? In central Virginia? Where there wasn't a streetlight for twenty miles? There could be *anything* out there just on the other side of the walls of our house, and it could be creeping up on our house, and it could even be peering into the windows of our house and we would have *no way* of knowing because it was so freaking dark!

I'd forgotten how dark it gets at night when there are no artificial lights. I'd forgotten how quiet it is where there are no bombs, car horns, or drunken Filipinos or vendors. Sure, I could hear the frogs in the pond in the front yard, and it was a welcome sound, and I could hear the crickets chirping, and their presence was welcome as well, but when both would go silent, and then a floorboard would creek as the house settled, or the tin roof would pop as it cooled in the night after having baked in the sun all day, I was out of bed, on my feet, and walking around to investigate with an aluminum baseball bat in my hands.

Eventually, and just a few nights later, I would finally accept the fact that I was where I was, and this is how the nights were where I was, and it's what I'd wanted, and not to fear it but to embrace it. In a word, I began sleeping like a baby by the end of the first week in our new (to us) house.

Until November.

When the winds of November came.

And brought something ominous and fearsome with them.

***

We settled into our new routine in our new home on our new land, relatively quickly. A lot of it simply had to do with the fact that we were worn out from our topsy turvy life of the past year. I'd spent six months, alone, in the U.S., getting Dearly's visa, we'd moved my family back in the Philippines three times during that time after getting word of kidnapping plots on my son in hopes of hefty ransoms, and then I'd gone back, stayed with my family in Manila for six months before coming to the U.S., together, and then renting for three months, appeasing the powers that be in the public school system, and then finally settling down on our homestead after moving in. It was literally our eighth move in a year, this is counting another time we moved while living in Manila, simply because my wife had picked a real shithole of a place to live there, right across from the mall of Asia, before I'd flown back to live with her and our son. It was a small room, about the size of a closet- the typical type of living arrangements made by many of the service workers in the area who work twelve hour days and merely need a small space to sleep when not working. This was not good for us, by my standards, so I'd moved us to Makati City, the most high end part of Manila, and we quite enjoyed our stay there for the five months we were there after having spent a month in the broom closet.

Though settled, we were still quite busy. Our son's school was nearly half an hour's drive away from our property and we were taking him there in the mornings and going and picking him up in the afternoons. Yes, there is a bus, and yes, he does ride it these days, but it took us that first year to get over the idea of someone constantly trying to kidnap him for ransom, so we were not about to let him out of our sight.

When we'd get home from picking him up from school in the afternoons, we'd often lay on air mattress out on the lawn, underneath one of our many walnut trees, for shade, because it was still September, and then October, and in our part of central Virginia, it is still quite hot that time of year. We would lay together, the three of us, and stare into our fields (which are now meadows, and quickly on their way to becoming a forest), and watch the deer and the rabbits. We've seen the occasional bear and turkey. So many hawks fly above our place, regularly, you'd think it was a bird of prey preserve. And there are far too many gray squirrels to count. Often, on these first afternoons at our new home, (and it was, *finally*, our home, after all those years of moving around due to poverty and safety) we would fall asleep in the field, on our air mattress, and wake up just in time to go inside, have dinner, and then fall asleep for the night in our bed.

Then, as if the winds had a calendar, just as it turned November 1, a few minutes after midnight, the winds whipped up something fierce, as they'd say here in the south, and my feeling of peace left and I was right back to where I'd been that first week in our home.

You see, as our land lay, and as the land around it lies, it makes for the perfect scenario for heavy winds. There is a small river down the road and over the hill from our property. It's about two hundred yards away. And all the land beside the road, once passing our property, is wooded. Our land is the first open land in the immediate area (it was formerly hay fields) so when the temperatures begin dropping drastically in November, and the water's temperature is actually higher than the air temperature around it, it creates a draft. And since the land around the river, except for the road, is all wooded, the easiest way for the draft to escape, and rise, as warm air does, is to come up the road. Then, once these warm drafts reach our property, they go batshit crazy, because they can, because they have the space. The winds (fyi, wind is defined as the result of the uneven heating and cooling of the earth's surface, in case you didn't know) then whip around like crazy on our six acres. It's as if they run around, playing tag with each other, until they spin themselves out.

Our old house has beautiful old eaves that hang over each window. They're angled perfectly for keeping the sun's direct shine out of the windows during the summer, but they allow for it to shine in during winter. . These were necessary when the house was built, because air conditioning, at the time, was a fantasy at most, as was heating systems outside of woodstoves and fireplaces. Neither had been invented yet. These days, the eaves are not necessary, but we leave them, because it helps our old house look more rustic. We feel like we're living in an antique, which I guess we are. The house is listed on the historical registry here in Virginia.

Anyway, the point to all of this is that as those winds on that first night of November reached our property, and then our house, they lifted these eaves above the windows, at least the ones upstairs, and then as the winds passed on, the eaves would drop back into their natural place and it sounded as if someone was jumping around in the upstairs bedrooms of our house.

When this first happened, I awoke with a start, immediately believing I was back in Mosul, Iraq, and that another s-vbied (suicide vehicle bourne improvised explosive devise) had rammed into the gate, killing all the guards and making a hole for an insurgent attack. I sat up, and I reached to the side of my bed to grab my M-4, but alas, it was not there. I jumped up, ready to find it, and that's when I saw my wife and our son sleeping in our custom made king sized bed, and I remembered where I was.

And then it happened again!

Another slam from upstairs convinced me someone was in the house. I may not have had an M-4 ready by my bed, but I did have an aluminum baseball bat that I keep there to this day for such events. For some reason, I've had a couple people out this way ask me if I have firearms. I had no idea why I was asked this at first, but I've since come to believe that they asked this because they are anti-gun types (yes, I'm out in the country, but it is right outside of a university town, and there are tons of those types out here), and they wanted to judge me as as 'gun nutter' had I said yes. I did not answer their question, and I will not answer it here, but what I told them was exactly where my bedroom window was located, and I challenged them to come climbing through it at 2 a.m. some night and find out.

They both (two different beta-males on two separate occasions), simply turned and walked away and never came back!

Anyway, I took my bat and I headed upstairs. I heard the slams a couple more times on my way up. They were coming from our son's room. He hadn't actually moved into his room yet, because allowing him to sleep with us that first year here, even though he was already in kindergarten, was part of our cooling down process as well. Let me tell you, when you have to spend the first five years of your kid's life worrying about them being kidnapped for ransom, because their father is a white foreigner living in a non-white third world country riddled with terrorists and common criminals, old habits are hard to break. However, we since have, and it's a really nice feeling being able to let our guards down just a bit.

The door to my son's room was open, and though the light was off, I could still see into the room quite well. We had not hung the blinds yet, and the moon happened to be almost full that night, and there wasn't a cloud in the sky, so the light from the moon was coming through the windows lighting the place up almost as if it were day.

As I was looking out the window, a gust picked up and slammed the eave again, and this time, I saw the actual movement of the eave, and I heard and felt the resulting slam, and I was immediately set to ease. I laughed at myself as I lowered the baseball bat from my shoulder.

But then I immediately raised it again!

As I was peering outside the window, I saw something large scurry around the side of our detached garage which sits outside and below the window. And what I'd seen was no animal on all fours. What I'd seen, for just a moment, was walking upright on two legs, and it was big.

Very big!

I didn't go to the window, knowing that I was far enough away from the window so that I could see out of it, but if anyone or anything was outside looking in they could not see me. If I were to get close to the window, whoever or whatever was out there would be able to see me.

I stood, motionless, for a minute, and realizing a drawn bat would be of no use to someone or something outside the window, I lowered it again, but I remained vigilant. A couple more minutes passed, during which time the eave outside the window banged and slammed a couple of more times, and then I saw it again.

Actually, two of them!

I could not believe what I was seeing at first, and I actually *did* move to the window this time to get a better view. What I saw completely blew my mind, and it would take me nearly a year to come to accept what it is that I saw, though I have to admit, that at the time, I believe I already knew.

At first, there was only one. One large, and I mean *really* large, creature, walking on two legs, away from the back of the detached garage and up the hill of what was then our upper field. It had recently been cut for hay, as we'd allowed the man who'd taken the hay from the land for years (the land had belonged to his mother's cousin before we bought it) take one last cut before using the land exclusively for our own purposes. The man was, and still is, a total dickbag, and my immediate instincts told me at the time that it was this very man, the annoying neighbor that I would eventually have to run off with a crayon, that I was seeing outside that night. I believed he was stalking us (because he actually did for a while), and that he was outside being a peeping tom (which he'd been fired from the University of Virginia for being, I would later find out), and I was about to run out the back door and give him a good, old fashioned Appalachiastanian hillbilly ass whoopin'!

But then, the first creature was joined by a second. This one was just a bit smaller, but it was still massive in size!

It occurred to me that these creatures were not men. They were not human, though they appeared to take human form. That is, as long as you consider professional NFL tight ends and WWE wrestlers. They had to be nearly eight feet tall, and if I were a betting man, which I'm not, because I've always been too good at math to gamble or play the lottery, I would wager they weighed close to eight hundred pounds.

I watched in awe as these two entities, slowly and methodically, while looking back on occasion, made their way to the top of the hill, about four hundred yards away, before slipping into the woods behind my house. I rubbed my eyes a few times as they made their way up the hill, and I even pinched myself once, and sure enough, I was fully awake, as I would remain the rest of the night, despite the winds of November finally dying down and the ceasing of the banging of the eaves.

As I lay in bed the rest of the night, I questioned my sanity. I mean, I knew I was messed up a bit from the war. I knew I was messed up due to my time in the Philippines, and the events that took place there. I knew I had issues due to personal losses resulting from both.

But I knew I wasn't crazy!

Well, that much.

But I knew what I'd seen!

It would take more experiences like this one, and it would later take confirmation from some really supportive and credible people on a YouTube channel we now have that did not exist at the time- that first fall that we were in our new home on our new property- but today I have every reason to believe I know exactly what I saw, and only for the first time, on that November night when I'd been awakened by the winds of November.

Potentially...

...two...

Bigfoot Sasquatch!

2

Bigfoot Sasquatch Saves The World

Okay, so I'm pretty open with my life on our YouTube channel "Homesteading Off The Grid." I'm open with my daily affairs, many of which are 'same 'ol, same 'ol,' and honestly, becoming boring. Splitting wood, mowing grass, growing weed gardens (no, not *that* kind of weed, and they're meant to be vegetable gardens, but if you miss a few days straight of weeding, the weeds get the better of you, and we have a tendency to miss a few *weeks* straight every year, so come harvest time, we're wading chest high in weeds looking for vegetables. It's much like an Easter egg hunt.). Oh, and going around the woods and meadows behind my house looking for him, her, it or they.

And I've been pretty open with much of my past. Mostly, by way of writing about it in my novels under the guise of fiction. Especially all those 'down and out years' in the Philippines.

"How did you go from being a batshit crazy, drunk, down and out disabled vet in the Philippines to an upper middle class Virginia landowner just outside of Charlottesville?" people often ask.

"Why," I begin in response, "by never giving up. I focussed on my writing, and in time, I got good at it. Eventually, I got on the map and the money started coming in, and we were able to leave the jungle and get back to the city, and a couple of years after that we were able to come to the U.S., and well, things were going so well that we were able to buy a house on six acres out in the country, just outside of Charlottesville, and well," I say, just like I started with, "everything just worked out."

"There seems to be some holes in your story," the most astute of naysayers will say.

"How so?" I'll ask.

"How did you survive?" they'll say. "During those *down and out years* as you call them. I mean, you had to be making money somehow. At least enough to sustain yourself and your *beautiful bride*, as you call her, and your son. How did you do it?"

At this point, I don't plead the fifth. But I come close. I refer my examiner to my novel, "Isle of Kapre," and I say to them, "good luck figuring out which part of the story is fact, and which part is fiction."

At this point, I'll get a look of confusion. However, I get no further questioning, because the people who tend to make it this far along in their inquisition do have a half a brain cell or two more than the average bear, and some of them actually do read the book. And of those who get back to me after reading the book? They all say the same thing.

"You really *are* batshit crazy!"

What's my point to all this? Well, it's simple, really. In my previous life, I made many contacts. Contacts in high places who relay messages through common friends in low places. If this sounds like I'm speaking (well, typing) in riddles, it's because I am, and it's for a reason.

"Why?" you ask.

Again, if you haven't read it, go read "Isle of Kapre," and you'll totally get it.

And you, too, will be convinced I'm batshit crazy if you're not already.

Anyway, here's what all this has to do with this story.

Be prepared for a validated, actual, bonafide, effective vaccine for Covid-19, no later than the end of February, 2021, if, indeed, it's not out by the time you read this book!

"What in the name of all things holy are you talking (well, typing) about now, Crazy Lake?" you might be asking yourself?

This!

***

Ring!

It was my cell phone. It was early on a Sunday morning in October of 2020. I'd planned to sleep in, because I'd been up late the night before doing a night hunt for Bigfoot Sasquatch in the woods behind my house, and making a video of it for my YouTube channel, as well as approving final edits for my most recent novella length collection of short stories, "Bigfoot Sasquatch Files Volume 5." It was a busy night, a night on which I was up well past midnight, and I was, as our friends in the U.K. would say, cream crackered! That means worn out in American.

I grabbed the phone and looked at the number calling. I sat straight up in bed, instantly wide awake, and I answered before it had a chance to ring a second time. The number calling was from an individual I'd never given my number to, but I guess guys like him have the ability to find you. Or anyone. Anywhere. The events that took place on the Isle of Kapre is proof enough of that.

"Yes, sir?" I said.

"You're not gonna believe this," the voice on the other side of the line said. It was the voice from a fifty year old man who was supposed to be dead.

"I'm kinda having a hard time believing you're still alive," I said.

"Remember," he said. "Believe nothing you hear and only half of what you see."

"Fuck you," I said.

"Why?" he said.

"I cried for a minute when I thought you were dead."

"Wow," he said. "A whole minute?"

"You think you're worth more time than that?"

"I love you, too, but we'll catch up later. I have a job for you."

"Um, do you know where I am?" I asked.

"Yes," he said. "You're sitting up in your bed in the downstairs master bedroom of your old sharecropper house out in the country, just outside of Charlottesville. You're staring at the far wall telling yourself you need to get around to painting it, and the rest of the inside of your house, again, because four winters worth of smoke from your woodstove has taken its toll on the last paint job."

"Did you mother fuckers put cameras up in my house?" I asked, the feeling of panic like I'd not felt in years instantly returning.

"No," he said, laughing. "I'm just fucking with you." He was laughing so hard it took him a hot second to be able to speak again. "Lucky guess, but look."

"Fuck you," I said, now feeling my heart rate coming back down.

"Okay, we're done with the fuck yous. You need to listen. I have a job for you. But yes, we know exactly where you live and how you live."

"How?" I asked, now looking around for pinhole sized camera lenses in the corners of the room.

"You broadcast your life on YouTube," he said.

"Oh," I said, feeling myself disarming again.

"Look," he said. "We need you to go back to the lair."

"What lair?" I asked.

"The lair of Bigfoot Sasquatch, you dumb fucker," he said.

"Are you serious?" I asked.

"It's either there or the Isle of Kapre," he said. "Take your pick."

"What do you," I began, but then I thought better of it and reworded my question. "What do *they* need from me now?"

"DNA," he said, short and sweet with no further explanation, and I'd worked with him enough in the past to know that he would give no further explanation so there was no need for me to press. And I didn't blame him. Guys who work in his capacity have a tendency to be disappeared for giving too much information, and frankly, guys like me who've performed certain 'odd jobs' in the past, like the odd jobs I was performing leading up to and even during my time spent on the Isle of Kapre had a tendency to be disappeared for knowing too much, too.

"Why me?" I asked. "I thought I was done. I thought that was part of the deal. I work for your guys once, and I get to come home and live happily ever after and all that bullshit. We got their man in office. We set up their puppet Government. We eliminated the threat from those networks these fucking know it all, pampered, smartest assholes in the room Americans over here have never even heard about, because we never allowed them and their actions to reach the scale of making mainsteam news, where all the smartest assholes in the room garner all their information."

"A little bitter, or just a lot?" he asked. "Let me know when you're done. If you'd like to persist, I can have my assistant run out and pick up some cheese to go along with your whine."

"Fuck you," I said.

"We're done with that," he said. "Remember?"

"What's in it for me?" I asked.

"You get to keep living your happily ever after," he said.

"And if I don't do it?" I asked, already knowing the answer.

"They're going to take it all away," he said. "Remember, what the large print giveth, the fine print taketh away."

And I knew there was no need to argue my case. Trust me, the people he contracted for had a way of not just disappearing people, but destroying people in such a way that makes them *wish* they'd disappeared, and it was the promises that they *didn't* renege on that always amazed me.

"Tell me what I need to do," I said, swinging my feet over the side of the bed, rising, and then heading into the kitchen to start the coffee while my informant gave me the mission.

***

When I've got shit to do, I have a tendency to get it done- like, now, not later- hence, only an hour after having my coffee and breakfast, I was off to go hiking through the woods behind my house, the potential lair of the potential Bigfoot Sasquatch being my final intended destination. I'd told my beautiful bride, Dearly, also known as 'Giggly Girl' on our YouTube channel, that I was burned out on running and cycling, and so my morning exercise was going to be hiking.

"You are going to da lair to make to da YouTube video?" she asked in her ever-cute and ever-broken English.

"Something like that," I said.

"Oh," she said. "Was that…" she trailed off.

"Yeah," I said.

"I thought he was dead?" she said.

"Guess not," I said, lacing up my hiking boots.

"I wish he dead," she said.

"That's not nice," I said.

"He not nice," she said.

"It's not his job to be nice," I said. "It's his job to get shit done so the world keeps spinning and the protected can remain protected, and bitch and complain about it the whole time because they have no fucking clue how protected they are."

"You go," she said. "Just don't bring any of that shit back with you."

By 'that shit," she meant anything of paranormal, supernatural, or cryptozoological nature, but little did she know, *shit* is exactly what I planned on bringing back with me. I had to. It was the mission. Shit contained DNA, and yes, I could have gone after saliva or hair, or even blood (which could have ended badly for me), but I'd made it my little personal prank on humanity to go after shit.

You see, I've been a manbrat/smartass bastard since the days of the old testament, my friends!

Two hours and a roughly five mile hike later, I'd reached my destination. I was, potentially, in the middle of the lair that may or may not have belonged to Bigfoot Sasquatch.

"Jesus," I said to myself, half a complaint rooted in a complete loss of knowing what to do now, and half in the form of an actual prayer. "What do I do now?"

No answer came to me, but I figured I'd just get to doing what I'd come to do. I slipped off my backpack, which is my old Army assault pack from Iraq, and I took out the pair of purple latex gloves I'd brought with me and slipped them on. I took out the half a dozen plastic grocery store bags I'd brought with me (which, by the way, are of the devil. They are pure evil. They are responsible for so much pollution and death of wildlife around the world. And I *do* mean around the world. I have seen plastic bags from Food Lion ((a major grocery store chain in the southern U.S.)) blowing around in the wind all over the world. I have seen these plastic bags blowing through the Arabian Desert in Iraq. I have seen them blowing along the beaches and through the jungles of Southeast Asia. Yes, actual plastic bags from Food Lion in the southern U.S.! I guess they caught some really intense upward heat drafts), and I began searching the forest floor all around me for shit.

Bigfoot Sasquatch shit!

"This is deer shit," I said aloud, finding my first pile of droppings. At first, I had no intentions of bagging up this deer shit and turning it into my superior (God, I hate referring to that asshole as my superior), but I figured that if I went back empty handed I'd be accused of not having tried hard enough, so, bag it up I did.

I continued walking around, slowly, and in pretty short order, I managed to bag up more deer shit, some racoon shit, some groundhog shit, and finally, after searching for nearly an hour, I found a big steaming pile of bear shit. Now, it was pretty easy for an experienced woodsman like me (yes, I'm an experienced woodsman, even though so many vertically challenged individuals who live under bridges accuse me of being a 'city boy' on our YouTube channel) to be able to tell that this was only bear shit, but I'd be able to use the excuse that it was so fresh that I couldn't tell, and that would get me a pass. At least long enough to get a second chance to come back.

Next, after having been awakened early by the phone call after a late night, and hiking for hours, and searching for shit, literally, for hours, I sat down, my back against a large red oak tree, and I fell asleep.

***

I don't know how long I slept, but when I woke up, I was ravishingly hungry. I immediately thought of the twinkies I'd brought in my assault pack. Realizing I was probably a good quarter mile away from my pack, I immediately got up and began walking back to my pack, making sure to take my bags of shit with me. I hurried the pace, because I was really, really hungry (yes, I know that's redundant, and it's intentional, because I want to really make the point about how hungry I was), and I really, really love twinkies.

Alas, as I got to within sight of my assault pack, only fifty yards away through the forest, I saw a scene that was heartbreaking. A large, dark figure was opening my assault pack, and I knew it was going to take my twinkies.

"You fucking bear!" I yelled, assuming that the thief was the black bear that had recently deposited the huge, steaming pile of shit I now held in the bag in my left hand. "Leave my twinkies alone, you fucking fuck!"

I began running at the thief, knowing that black bears are relatively docile creatures, and that they, like all wild animals (except wild hogs, which, fortunately, are only found considerably further south of where I live) fear humans more than anything.

Once I'd cut the distance between myself and my assault pack and the large, hairy thief in half, I stopped in my tracks. I nearly deposited my own steaming pile of that which I was carrying in my plastic Food Lion grocery bags, because what stood before me, on two legs, not four, was no black bear.

It was…

…potentially…

…Bigfoot Sasquatch!

"Oh, shit," I said.

The creature let out a mighty roar. Then, while holding my now open assault pack with one hand, it jammed its other hand inside it and pulled out, not my twinkies, but…

...wait for it...

...a spicy Italian sub on flatbread from Subway that I'd bought and forgotten to eat more than a month before. It had been in one of the different pouches on my assault pack that I'd not checked before leaving for my hike because I'd been in such a hurry. I mean, I was doing the job as a subcontractor for a guy who was doing his job as a subcontractor for a group of people who are not known for their patience, so I simply hadn't taken the time to check all the pouches, even though I could smell quite a stench. A stench like that made by rotten meat.

"Argh!" the creature yelled again, like a big hairy pirate, and if I were to translate what the 'argh' meant, I mean, with my morning phone conversation still fresh in my mind, I would have reason to believe that the 'argh' meant, "fuck you!" The beast crammed the entire sub of rotten meat and wilted vegetables into his, her or its mouth, wrapper and all, and gave me a hard stare, that I would equally translate into a 'fuck you,' and then it dropped my assault pack and then turned and ran over the mountainside with such speed it was gone instantly.

I hurried to my assault pack, and fortunately, my twinkies, all of them, were still in it. I took the twinkies out of my assault pack and I ate of them. And I became full of the twinkies that were in my assault pack. And I was pleased by the feeling of being filled of the twinkies that had been in my assault pack all was good with the world.

***

"Shit," I said, walking back down the mountain after having finished my twinkies. "Now what?" Again, it was part complaint and part prayer.

But this time, the answer came to me in the way of a moan. A moan emanating from the middle of a laurel thicket about one hundred yards to my right. I stopped, I listened, and I was pleased!

Bigfoot Sasquatch had eaten a rotten Italian sub from Subway! Bigfoot Sasquatch had a terrible tummy ache as a result of a mild case of food poisoning!

Bigfoot Sasquatch had the shits!

My job had just become simple. All I had to do was wait, and wait was all I did. I hunkered down beside a large poplar tree, and I was conveniently hidden behind my own thicket of laurel, and it was all I could do to not laugh my ass off while listening to the large, bipedal beast shitting his, her or its guts out only a hundred yards away. I mean, I wasn't trying to be mean, taking pleasure in his, her, or its pain, but Karma is real. You steal a man's food, you get a case of the shits, right? And besides, the creature could have been lucky enough to have opened the other pocket on my assault pack and stolen my twinkies. Then where would I be? Would I have eaten the spoiled sub? Would I be the one with the shits now? I mean, I *am* batshit crazy, so maybe.

Anyway, after a quarter of an hour or so, the beast seemed to be finished, and I knew that out here in the wild, there was no paperwork to do, so once it (or him, or her) crept further down the hill after making its deposit, I waited another fifteen minutes or so to make sure it was gone, and then I went to the laurel thicket where it (or him, or her) had made its extremely large deposit.

I'd hit the mother load!

Knowing this was exactly what I'd come for, I dumped out all the other shit I'd already collected- deer shit, raccoon shit, bear shit- and I'd even found what I thought was bat shit, and I almost kept that as a suveigner, you know, because I'm told it's the type of crazy I am? But no! I needed all the room in my plastic bags I could get, so I dumped out the bat shit, too. Once my bags were all shit free, I reloaded them, this time with nothing but shit from him, her, it, or... well, there was only one, so there was no they. And then I headed off the mountain, considering this yet another successful mission. I felt elated, because I'd not actually performed any type of missions for these guys since leaving Mindanao more than five years ago. Even though I hated the bastards, familiar territory felt good.

***

Here's what I can tell you about the outcome of my mission. I left the 'package' where I was instructed to leave it, and where I'm sure it was picked up the second I was out of sight.

Like all my missions, I'm never told the exact specifics, or, like I discussed earlier, any specifics, but I always have my hypothesis, and here's my hypothesis in regard to this mission:

I know this mission was carried out during the peak days of the Covid-19 virus. Further, I know that the amount of DNA similarities that we share with him, her, it or they are so close it would terrify most people, especially all those know it all smartest assholes in the room who believe these creatures don't exist, anyway, because, well, mainstream media has never confirmed their existence, and that's where they garner all their information.

Further, I have reason to believe that there are no such things as 'new viruses.' I believe that everything is cyclical. I believe that this Covid-19 virus has visited us before, however, it did so during the days before we were nearly as advanced as we are today, and I don't mean only in regard to science and medicine. I mean in regard to record keeping, as well. I believe this virus, and many others, visited us thousands of years ago, and I do believe that it wiped out large populations.

However, I also believe that large populations developed herd immunity to the virus, and I believe that the Bigfoot Sasquatch population happens to be one of those populations.

And I believe the people who subcontracted me for this mission, through a subcontractor, knew this, hence this mission.

So, like I said, look for the 'miracle vaccine' within ninety days of the publishing of this story, unless, like I also said, it's here already, before this story even has time to be published.

Oh, and I got word a couple days after completing this mission that my contact died in a single car vehicular accident.

I'm sure I'll hear from him again. As soon as *they* want something from me again.

Oh, and know, that when you receive the vaccine for Covid-19, should you choose to, or, should we all be forced to...

...wait for it...

...you're (potentially) being shot up with a big 'ol steaming dose of Bigfoot Sasquatch shit!

The End

3

The Things We Leave Behind

"Ya'll ain't never gonna see it, what, with the piss poor attitudes ya'll have about it."

It was Herb. He wasn't *really* a cop, but they let him wear the uniform and walk the streets- not drive the cruiser, mind you, but walk. And they let him have a billy club, but not a handgun.

"Shoot, what with the piss poor attitudes ya'll boys have about everything."

"Ah, come on, Herb," my childhood best friend, Ricky said. "Just tell us exactly where it is so we can go see it. We just want a glimpse." We were thirteen years old and had nothing better to do than to harass the man we viewed as the town's fool.

"Now, I ain't tellin' ya'll boys where it is. I know ya'll better than you *think* I do. Why, you're liable to go up there and try to shoot it," Herb said. And he was right. If he told us where it was, that's *exactly* what we were going to do. We were going to go into the woods, up on the hill behind Herb's house, which overlooked our entire small town, and we were going to kill us a Bigfoot Sasquatch, and we were going to become rich and famous for doing so.

But really? We didn't believe any of Herb's stories, so more than anything, we were going to debunk him.

"Now, that time I went and told ya'll boys about where the spaceships were landin', ya'll went up there with your flashlights, and your tent, and you built your bonfire, and they ain't been back!"

Herbs thing, for years, when Ricky and I had been younger, had been aliens and U.F.O.'s. He'd claimed he knew where their landing strip was. At least the one in our area, where they would park their ship while visiting and taking samples of the lifeforms that lived in our area.

"They don't hurt nothin' that breathes," Herb used to go on and on, back in those days. "They only want to study our plantlife. Why, they know how harmful them meats are to a body, so they don't touch it." Herb had claimed to become a vegetarian after having not just observed the aliens he claimed to see from afar, but after having, or at least he claimed, conversed with them telepathically. "Why, they don't even waste time and energy with speakin'," he'd told us back then. "They do it all mentally. Inside their heads."

We'd actually gotten Herb to tell us the specific location of this alleged (or, potential) U.F.O. landing area, and we had gone camping up there, and though we never saw any U.F.O.'s or strange lights in the night sky, we *did* find an area that looked as if it had been burned up in a forest fire. It was only the size of a basketball court. Nothing big at all. And there were several very strange indentations in the soil in the area, as if something large and heavy had sat in the area. We wrote it all off to Herb trying to set us up. Make us believe his idiotic story about the U.F.O.'s. I mean,we knew he was our village idiot. At least that's what we'd thought at the time.

"I can only imagine how bad things would have been back then," Herb said, reflecting on the night that Ricky and I had gone camping at his alleged (or, potential) U.F.O. landing pad, "if ya'll'd been totin' around firearms like ya'll are nowadays."

I'll tell you this, here and now, and just by way of being honest when looking back on it. Herb was right. Had any unidentified flying objects come around Ricky and me back in the day (circa 1987), we would have shot them out of the sky.

But that was a long time ago.

A very long time ago.

In time, Ricky and I would outgrow our infatuation with passivily aggressively harassing the man we viewed as the town's idiot by listening to his tall tales about aliens and Bigfoot Sasquatch. We would discover a new infatuation.

Girls!

We started chasing them shortly after giving up on getting
Herb to let us in on the specific location of this alleged (or,
potential) Bigfoot Sasquatch that he claimed lived in the
woods behind his house. Herb soon became an afterthought.
He would become that weirdo we'd see walking up and down
the sidewalk in front of the theater (this being back when our
little town in Appalachiastan had not yet become the meth and
pill riddled shithole that it is today, like so many small towns in
Appalachiastan that once thrived before the days of the
internet), one hand on his holstered billy club, the other on his
pants waist, opposite side the billy club, in order to hold them
up, because they were a size too large. The department was
not going to put in an order for a new uniform for a guy who
was merely an 'honorary policeman' as they called him.

"There's the guy that claims to see aliens and Bigfoot
Sasquatch," Ricky and I would whisper to our dates as we
prepared to pass Herb on our way to see the latest Friday the
13'th installment, or the newest Rocky or Indiana Jones. Ricky
or I, or both of us, would make some sort of snide comment to
Herb about the claims he'd made to us when we were
younger. He'd put his head down and act like he hadn't heard
us, and our dates would tell us we were mean and they would
never go out with us again. It took us a while to learn that girls,
the good ones, at least- the ones worth keeping- didn't view
being mean to other people, especially those who came
across as weaker-than, as a turn on.

Ricky and I grew up, and this is the point in which most stories
would read that we went our separate ways and conquered
the world, but it's not how this story goes. I left that little

Appalachian town and I went on to college, and after graduating, I left Appalachiastan entirely.

Ricky didn't.

He never got out.

And neither of us conquered the world. The world would eventually conquer Ricky, and me? Well, let's just say I'm still fighting.

Ricky wasn't the brightest tool in the shed. At least that's how we'd referred to him as kids. As it turns out, he suffered from dyslexia and a very mild case of Aspergers. We just thought he struggled with reading and was funny as shit- the guy willing to say the things the rest of us weren't- but I guess we were wrong.

Ricky stayed behind, and as the middle class fled Appalachiastan, beginning in the mid-nineties, as a result of the then, newly internet driven economy- an economy that allowed for people to work from home, hence, allowing them to work from anywhere- Ricky's economic options began to shrink. He'd barely graduated high school, and the only jobs he could get were labor jobs. He'd started out doing okay in the coal mines, but with the restrictive regulations President Clinton would put on mining, causing many of the mines back in Appalachiastan to close, Ricky would soon find himself unemployed and unemployable at the ripe old age of twenty six.

However, a new industry was taking over much of Appalachiastan.

Methamphetamine!

As the infomercials we all grew up watching in the 80's would put it, Ricky would not just become the president of his own little meth lab and distribution business, he would also become a client. And he would soon begin his vicious cycle of jail, court ordered rehab, the street. Jail, court ordered rehab, the street.

Like so many addicts in Appalachiastan, or hell, anywhere else in the world for that matter, everyone who knew Ricky would soon distance themselves from him. His family, friends, and sadly, even me, wrote him off as dead, though, for a while, he was still very much alive. It was a mix of not wanting to be associated with him and loving him too much to watch him continue to kill himself slowly, as addiction is basically a form of suicide on installment.

But not Herb.

Herb always saw Ricky as that smartass little ten year old who wanted to know where the U.F.O.'s landed. Then, as that smartass thirteen year old who wanted to go and shoot himself a Bigfoot Sasquatch and become famous for doing so. And later, as that older teen who was feeling his oates so rowdy that he'd say the occasional mean thing he didn't really mean, in the hopes of impressing a beautiful member of the opposite sex.

Herb never had the validated capacity to arrest Ricky, and he never did. But there had been many a night when Herb had spent the night with Ricky in the drunk tank. There were so many times that Herb would catch a ride to the regional jail with whatever officer was taking someone up for their next stay, and he would visit with Ricky while there, the other officer- the *real* officer- processing the new intake while he did.

Herb would visit with Ricky in his cheap, no-tell hotel room that he could rent for twenty dollars a night (and sometimes the heating system in the room actually worked in the winters) on those rare occasions that Ricky was not locked up in either jail or rehab. On more than one occasion Herb allowed Ricky to stay with him when he didn't have a twenty to rent his room and no one else would. This is how it went all the way up until about ten years ago. Until Herb died at the ripe old age of eighty three.

Then Ricky had absolutely no one.

No one knew the specifics, but Ricky got himself stabbed to death about a month ago. He was forty five years old. The surprising part of the whole thing is that everyone was shocked he'd actually lived *that* long. It was a given assumption that Ricky probably died due to a drug deal. Either he'd bought and not paid, or he was selling to someone who had no intentions of paying. Either way, most folks thought, it was for the better. And not just for the community, but for Ricky. Everyone viewed it as if he was merely a suffering animal being put out of its misery.

But not me.

I cried when I got the news.

I hadn't spoken with or communicated online with Ricky for more than a decade. It broke my heart to do it, but what I'll say is, to this day, I feel it had to be that way. You see, I may have left Appalachiastan, but none of us, anywhere, are free from the threat of addiction to the things that make us feel good. Especially, if for some reason, we have an addictive personality, the addiction gene, or, if we merely mess around with the wrong things for too long.

I've struggled myself, off and on, and I have reason to believe I always will, though each day I pray the struggle is over, and that true freedom from addiction has arrived, but experience has shown me that it's a back and forth battle I may never win, but I swear, God as my witness, I will *never* give up fighting. The point here is that not only did I have to distance myself from Ricky because I didn't want to be associated with him and because I loved him too much to continue watching him kill himself, but I had to distance myself from him in order to have a better chance of staying clean and sober myself.

I once had almost a year sober, and Ricky came up to see me. It was my last year in college, and I'll admit that I hadn't really dried out in order to stay dry, but to finish my senior year and graduate. Ricky and I went out and celebrated getting together for the first time in a long while. We got blackout drunk for a week, and I missed class for a week, and I ended up having to spend another semester in school because I'd failed a class, and I didn't see another sober day for several years.

Later in life, Ricky was the one actually trying to get straight. He had six months clean and sober, and who do you think went back to our little shit hole town in Appalachiastan to do some fly fishing? Why, me, of course, and I had to go see my old friend Ricky, and I just happened to have a case of beer with me, because when you go fishing, if you don't end up catching any fish, the least you can do is end up catching a buzz, and Ricky and I got shitfaced all week, and I never even *went* fishing, and a month after I left that shithole little town in Appalachiastan, Ricky would get his first of *many* D.U.I.'s.

And this is how it went for many years. When Ricky was straight, I'd take him back through the narrows. When I was dry, he'd wet me up.

We were no longer good for each other.

So, painfully, we parted ways, and I was the one who'd made that painful decision for both of us.

I didn't attend Ricky's funeral, and I doubt many people did. But the weight of the pain of our relationship weighed on me heavily, and finally, about two weeks ago, I took a day and drove back into that shithole town in Appalachiastan. Well, not really "into" as much as "on the outskirts of." You see, this is where the cemetery is.

I found Ricky's grave and I smirked and laughed lightly at the irony that it was so close to Herb's. They weren't next to each other. There were a few other graves in between them, but they were close enough to where you could see one while sitting beside the other. And that's what I did. I would sit by Ricky's, having telepathic conversations, in my head, with him *and* Herb (remembering Herb's aliens and laughing about it), and then I would move over to Herb's and do the same from there.

I caught myself reading the inscription on Herb's tombstone. I don't know why I didn't at first. I guess my mind was elsewhere. And I guess I just always viewed him as the village idiot, and I assumed the inscription on his tombstone would simply read that he was the village idiot.

Boy, was I wrong!

The inscription on Herb's tombstone was quite lengthy, and I read it all, and to sum it up in fewer words than were written, Herb was a hero!

Herb had served in the United States Army during World War Two. He'd been an airborne infantryman, and he was part of the group that stormed the beach at Normandy on D-Day. Then, he spent months fighting his way all across Europe, finally reaching Hitler's 'Crow's Nest,' and he was part of the group that delivered the final death blow to the Nazi regime.

"Wow!" I said aloud after having read the inscription. I looked up, skyward, to say a prayer for both of my fallen friends, and as I did, and as my eyes connected with the skyline, where the top of the hill met the sky, I saw something large, something dark, dart behind a large tree.

It was early November, and the leaves had already fallen from the trees. Whatever it was that I saw was a couple of miles away from me, but it could easily be seen because of the lack of leaves, and also because its sheer size.

I'd grown up in these mountains, and I'd seen plenty of black bears in my day. Large ones. But there is no such thing as a black bear as large as what I'd seen dart behind that tree. I watched, and I waited, but I did not see it again. Eventually, my curiosity got the better of me and I left the cemetery, and I went hiking.

Ironically, the closest place to the location where I'd seen something large and dark dart behind a tree on top of the mountain overlooking the cemetery, and the entire town, for that matter, was by way of Herb's back yard.

***

I didn't go to my car and drive to the other side of town to hike up the hill to see if I could get a better look at what I thought I'd seen. And I didn't even run. I walked. Slowly.

The town was small, and it had eroded since I'd left a quarter of a century ago. I ambled through what was once downtown, now a ghost town, and through the neighborhood on the opposite side of the town as the cemetery, receiving suspicious glares from the few people I saw as I did, until I reached Herb's old house. He'd been dead and gone a while now, and his house looked just as abandoned and dilapidated as so many of those surrounding it and just like so many of those that I'd passed on my way through the small hamlet.

This was the kind of place where when one died, and their beneficiaries inherited their property, their beneficiaries did *not* rejoice. There was no value to a crap house that could not sell, because there was nothing in the area to draw people in. And to use as a rental? Good luck! A revolving door of druggies and drunks who never pay rent and which require court orders that take nearly a year to obtain to evict. To inherit anything in this near third world shithole community is a burden, not a blessing, and it was no surprise to me that Herb's house had been allowed to merely fall apart at the hands of time, erosion, and a one hundred percent lack of care and upkeep.

I made my way through Herb's front yard, and then the back, and finally, into the woods. It took only twenty five minutes to hike to the top of the hill which overlooked the small community. Once on top, I found a large boulder that I'd known well in my childhood, and I sat on it, and I peered out over the once middle class community that now was just one little spot of existence in the great meth and opioid belt of Appalachia that has replaced what was once referred to as the rust belt. No, the industrial, labor type jobs never came back after the advent of computer technology, and for some reason the folks in the area never got on board with the new economy, and when there was no prosperity rushing in, the pills and the powders filled the void.

As I sat, attempting to shed tears for Ricky and Herb, tears that would not come, I fondled the pint of Jim Beam I had on the inside pocket of my coat. When I'd left home, it had not been cold, but I knew temperatures would be much lower here in the hills of Appalachiastan, and I'd been right, and I was thankful for the decision to have brought the coat, but I was wrestling with the decision I'd made about the bottle. I'd told myself I was going to have one last drink with Ricky, right there at his gravesite. I would take a swig, and then dump a shot on Ricky's grave. I'd take another swig and then give another to the earth that covered my old friend from whom I'd been estranged for the last decade of his life.

I was lying to myself again and I knew it. Rather, my disease, the only disease that spends its entire existence trying to convince those that have it that they do *not* have a disease, addiction, was whispering in my ear. The disease was doing the lying, and I was believing it. The diseases' lie went; *come on. It's a special occasion. You're drinking to the loss and memory of two old friends. It's just this once. Besides, you're giving half the bottle to the grave, so it's not like you're going to drink the whole pint.*

I pulled the bottle from my coat pocket, and as I held it in my left hand, I began to unscrew the lid with the fingers on my right.

"To Ricky," I said aloud.

And to Herb.

I turned quickly, assuming someone was standing right behind me, but no one was there. And with the realization that no one was there also came the realization that I'd not actually heard the words spoken. At least not aloud. I'd heard them in my mind.

Telepathically!

I stopped twisting the lid. I'd broken the seal, but I'd not taken the lid off. I lay it on the boulder I'd been sitting on and I began creeping around the woods, only in close proximity to where I already was. Though the leaves were off the trees, the mountain laurel for which Appalachiastan is famous was still out in its full evergreen bloom, so there could have been someone or something within only a few yards of me and it, or they, would be able to remain well hidden.

After getting about twenty yards away from the boulder where I'd been sitting, I began to hear weeping, and I did not hear it telepathically. I heard it here, in the physical realm. Someone, or some*thing*, was crying in the forest, but just as quickly as I'd caught the sounds of weeping, they disappeared. They hadn't lasted long enough for me to draw a bead on their exact location.

"I'm being emotional," I said to myself, and then I made my way back to the boulder where I'd been sitting. I took up the bottle and I sat down, and once again, I stared out across what I was now convinced was the precipice of my insanity.

"Ricky," I said, only a whisper.

"Herb," I heard, and the spoken word- spoken, by the way, in a very rough, guttural, almost growl sort of way- came from no more than ten yards to my right. I chose to ignore it, convinced I was losing my mind. It was my disease talking to me. I knew it's language well. I've heard it speak to me for many, many years. Since the time of my first drink many, many years ago. I knew that "Herb" actually translated to "hurry the fuck up and open that bottle and fucking feed me, you pussified mother fucker!"

I twisted the cap and took it off. I didn't even need to hold the bottle to my nose to smell the fumes of the sweet poison the bottle contained. My mouth began watering, instantly, and I felt my hands begin shaking. I instantly thought of those mornings after, when my hands would shake so wildly I couldn't put sugar in my coffee without spilling half of it from the spoon and onto the counter.

But that won't come until tomorrow, the disease whispered to me. And like 'ol Bob Seagar said, it continued. We've got tonight!

"You first, Ricky," I said, and I held the bottle up and out in front of me, using it like a site on a rifle, drawing a bead on which grave I thought might be Ricky's approximately a mile and a half away and at about three hundred feet lower in elevation. "For you, old friend."

I dumped half the contents of the bottle on the ground. Back in the day, during my active drinking days, I would call such an act alcohol abuse. But I was dumping out half, immediately, for Ricky, because I was going to pull on the rest of the bottle, hard, and drink the entire other half of the bottle in one fell swoop. I'd been clean and sober a number of years at this time, and I figured if I was going to go back to my old ways, I was going to do it right. I'd slam this half a pint into my blood system almost immediately, stagger out of the woods and to my car, and then get a case of beer at the local shithole convenient store and lock myself into a shithole no-tell motel room, hell, maybe even the one Ricky used to stay in, and I'd leave Appalachiastan at some point later.

Maybe…

And maybe in handcuffs or in a pine box.

But this mattered not to my disease, for it merely wanted fed.

And it mattered not to me at the time. I'd lost two friends I'd been out of contact with for years. This was my justification.

I hung my head and cried. It wasn't a light weeping, it was a full blown crybaby bawl. I held the bottle out and away from me, and I kept it steady, so I would not spill its precious contents, and that's when someone, or something, took it from my hand.

It took me a hot second to realize what had happened, and the instant I *did* realize what had happened, I heard the snapping of a stick only two feet away from me. This was *not* my crazy mind. This was *not* my disease. And this was *not* a sound that had been delivered telepathically.

This was real.

I raised my head, and I opened my eyes, but all that was before me was blurry. It was the first time I'd had a good cry in many years, and I guess my tears had been building up for some time, and when I'd finally had my cry, it was as if tiny dams had burst at the inner corners of my eyes, and for the *life* of me, all that I could see before me were blurry images. Shades, really.

The shade that stood out most was a large, dark shade smack dab in front of me and only two feet away. This shade was every bit of eight feet tall, and this shade was shaped like a WWE superstar. The shape extended what appeared to be an arm out to its side and it tipped over the bottle that it had taken from me.

"To Herb," the shape said as it dumped out the remainder of the bottle's contents.

I rubbed my eyes fiercely. My coat was still unzipped from where I'd opened it to pull the bottle out of my inside pocket. I reached in and grabbed my shirt and quickly brought it to my eyes to wipe away the tears. I rubbed hard, and when I took my shirt away from my face, my tears were gone, but now all was blurry from the pressure with which I'd rubbed my eyes.

But I could see clearly enough to see it!

There, about twenty yards away from me and heading into the laurel thickets was the dark shape I'd seen. The dark shape that had taken the bottle from me and dumped its contents to the ground in memory and honor of our old, mutual friend Herb. As the dark shape slipped away into the obscurity of the laurel thicket, my vision cleared just enough to where I could get one, crisp, clear view of what this shape truly was, and it was…

…potentially…

Bigfoot Sasquatch!

***

This story I've just told happened several weeks ago as of this writing. I'm happy to report that after what may or may not have been an actual (well, at least a *potential*) Bigfoot Sasquatch slipped out of my life, the thoughts of having that drink, for now at least, have done the same.

I managed to make my way off the mountain and out of the woods without incident. I weaved my way back through Herb's old neighborhood and through the streets of that old shithole, drug infested Appalachiastanian town, and I got into my car and made my way back home.

I've gotten back in touch with several of my *new* friends where I live now. Friends that have healthy, clean lifestyles. Friends with whom it's good and healthy for me to spend my time. But I *do* pray, daily, for those with whom I had to part ways simply out of the sheer necessity to stay alive, some of them living, but some of them gone far too soon.

And I continue to fight.

Daily.

The demons…

The End

4

In The Beginning

God created the heavens and the earth…

Wrong book.

This is the book of Bigfoot Sasquatch!

The sixth in this series, actually.

But before there was Bigfoot Sasquatch, there was…

Kapre…

And it's not about which came first, the chicken or the egg. The Bigfoot Sasquatch or the Kapre.

Let me explain.

I tell this story, one I've told more than once on our YouTube channel, "Homesteading Off The Grid," because I want it preserved in writing. When I began this venture, this 'Bigfoot Sasquatch Files," venture, I had no idea it would become a venture. Honestly, I thought I'd merely be wasting more time, spilling out more of my talents onto the page, only to have it fall on deaf ears, rather, no ears.

I've got too many carts before the horse here, so let me move them out of our way, one by one.

Firstly, I've worked in social media for more than a decade, and what I can tell you about the folks who spend a lot of time on social media, and who comment on posts often, are often fake. They are bored, they have nothing better to do with their time, and they piss endless hours of their days away scrolling, scrolling, scrolling. A good number of them use fake profiles so they can troll, or, and this is the true minority, simply remain anonymous (and if they're not trolling maliciously, I see no harm in this. It's actually a good idea for many reasons). My point here, in regard to the fakeness, at least, is that many of the comments they leave are left merely so they can 'look good.' They're not sincere.

At least this is what I thought.

Before my beautiful bride Dearly, who we know as Giggly Girl on YouTube, (because that's what she does. She giggles. Incessantly. And it's quite contagious), and I was successful on YouTube, we had success for a number of years on Fakebook. Most of you will know this social media platform as Facebook, but we've come to call it Fakebook, because it's as fake as it gets. From the users, which I described above, to the founder and owner, Mark Zuckerburg, who's all about promoting privacy and ethics, until someone like China waves some money in front of his face, at which time he waves the ethics he never had in the first place and sells China all of his Fakebook user's private information.

So, for many years, while we worked on Fakebook, and after I'd publish a book, the subscribers on our pages would shout, "If you make this book available in print, I'll buy a copy." I bought this hook, line and sinker, as hundreds of people said this, and after making my books available in print, I might sell four or five copies. The way the math actually worked, was that I would sell nearly one hundred e-copies of my books for every single print copy. But I would buy the lies, the fakeness, hook line and sinker, and go through the extra efforts, and back then, the extra costs associated with making my books available in print, only to be duped time after time after time.

So I eventually stopped.

But not so with our YouTube audience.

I'd not made any of my new books available in print for years by the time we became successful on YouTube after having left Fakebook. Once again, however, the commenters began clamoring, "If you'd write a book about Bigfoot Sasquatch, and make it available in print, we'd buy it." I ignored this for more than a year and a half, but after hearing it so much for so long, I finally decided to test the waters again, for the first time in years, and man, am I glad I did.

This is a big kudos, I guess, to our YouTube followers. These folks are not fake, like those Fakebook bastards. I was completely floored when, as a test, I put together a novella length collection of short stories for 'Bigfoot Sasquatch Files Volume 1' and made it available in print, and saw that our YouTube followers were actually putting their money where their mouths are. I mean, to put it bluntly, this whole 'Bigfoot Sasquatch Files' venture as I'm not referring to it, has given my family and me a second income stream that competes with our YouTube revenues. That was never the objective. We'd never even considered it as a goal. But we're flabbergasted that it's happened, and you'd better believe I plan on hanging on to this tiger's tail for quite some time to come. And not out of greed. We know enough about social media platforms to know that they may view you as one of their darlings one day, but should the winds of what's politically correct or socially cooth, or not, change, they have no problem killing their darlings, so having an active, profitable plan B in place is a nice thing, and it's brought us quite a bit of peace of mind.

Besides, and as I've said on our channel over and over and over. When you do what you love, you'll never work a day in your life. And I absolutely, profoundly, and as much as I love anything else in life (except my wife and our son), I love writing. It's my mistress. I can tell her anything, and she loves to listen, and she doesn't judge. She appreciates my honesty, and she doesn't care about the occasional fucking bad words. She doesn't tell me Jesus is coming to judge me first, and some of that other stupid shit the verically challenged individuals who live under bridges of the world constantly tell me on social media. She simply listens. And she accepts.

Okay, that went a little overboard, but my point is, our YouTube users are real, so as much for myself and my love of my mistress, writing, these Bigfoot Sasquatch Files collections will continue!

Now, the next cart in front of the horse.

The Kapre.

Now that I know these stories are being preserved in print (ah, the reason for my recently completed rant), I want to get my story of my night with the Kapre on paper. For you see, it was the experience which I'll now describe, for the first time, in print, that would lead to the creation of my novel "Isle of Kapre" and I do believe, open the door, if not a portal, or a slip in the veil, on our property in Virginia, years later, that would allow for the entire Bigfoot Sasquatch stuff we have going on (potentially), anyway.

Trust me.

It'll all make sense by the end.

***

To say that my beginning with the Potential Bigfoot Sasquatch only dates back to the events I'm about to describe- events that took place on a white, sandy beach in Southeast Asia, rather than the rugged, hemlock and giant western cedar studded Cascade Mountains of the Pacific Northwest, would be a lie. My beginning would actually start with a fascination with all things cryptic, paranormal, horrific and out of this world in childhood that I directly correlate to my mother's decision to allow me to watch the movie 'The Exorcist' when I was four years old. Since that dreaded night of terror, I became a firm believer in all things that could not be seen with the nake eye, be it demonic possession or large, hairy manlike beasts roaming the forests of the world.

But I'll take you to that white sandy beach of Mindanao, the southernmost island in the Philippines- an island riddled with mysteries and terrorist organizations (I'm telling you, if you haven't read 'Isle of Kapre' you don't' know what supercalifragilisticexpialidocious fiction based on *fact* is all about) in order to relate this particular tale of all things Bigfoot Sasquatch, well, at least all things closely related to Bigfoot Sasquatch (as in first cousins, perhaps, and you'll understand this, soon, too), because this is the tale of my first, up close and personal experience with, potentially, one of these amazing creatures that may or may not exist.

So, to give you the quick backstory in a paragraph or less, the year was 2011, and I'd recently returned to the Philippines after unsuccessfully securing proper employment in the U.S. I would spend the next four years straight there, after having gone back and forth, for several months at a time in each place, for the previous two years. I had a nine month old son there, Daniel, and a beautiful soul mate, Dearly, and it would be a long, hard four years of work, work, work, in the realm of literature and social media, creating something out of nothing, in order to get home (the U.S.) and be able to afford to live here.

During my first month back in the Philippines full time, Dearly and I got her aunt Marissa to keep our son for a night so we could take a fisherman's boat to a small island a couple miles off the coast of Mindanao in order to spend the night at a private resort. And don't think that's anything fancy. As I described in the previous paragraph, we were broke. But for two U.S. dollars, you could sleep in a bamboo shack without amenities pretty much anywhere on the beaches of the Philippines, and as long as it was a place away from where you usually stayed, it felt like a vacay.

We'd gotten to the other island late, as in an hour before dark, and the place where we wanted to stay had no vacancies, so we had to keep going up the beach. We found quickly that all the huts at all the small, privately owned properties had sold out for the night. We would soon be facing a very uncomfortable dilemma as the last boat to head back to Mindanao had already left for the evening. We were facing being stuck on this small island with no place to go.

Fortunately, just before nightfall (which comes at 5:30 p.m. in the Philippines, 365 days a year, as they're only seven degrees above the equator), we reached what seemed to be the end of the rocky, upward sloping road we'd been travelling by way of a rickety old tricycle (motorcar attached to the side of a moped), and there was a little old woman closing and locking a gate to a property on the side of the road, getting ready to go home for the evening. It would literally be dark in about ten minutes.

Dearly jumped off the tricycle and ran to the old woman and asked her if we could rent a hut for the night. The woman explained that their huts were only available for day rental and that no one ever spent the night at this resort, which lay at beach level about two hundred yards down a rocky trail. Dearly explained that we had nowhere else to stay, and the woman then explained to Dearly that the place was haunted. "Many Aswang," I heard her say. I didn't speak the Visayan language fluently yet, though I would in time, but I knew what 'Aswang' meant. It meant 'paranormal.'

"Cool!" I said, jumping off of the tricycle myself now and running over to the old woman. The old woman begged and begged us not to stay at the haunted resort, but I insisted.

When I offered her two hundred pesos, roughly four U.S. dollars, her eyes grew big and she unlocked the gate and told us to take any hut that we wanted. However, she said she would be locking us in for the night, and that a guard would be showing up soon (he should have been there by then, but finding anyone in the Philippines who's ever on time is like finding a needle in a haystack), and that he would be the only one around for a mile. This, I know now, but I did not know at the time, should have let me know how scared the locals were of this location. I mean, if you see ten square meters of free space in the Philippines, you'd better store the spot to memory, because within minutes, they'll have a dozen plywood shacks built on it with fifty people living there. And this is said with no disrespect. The place is severely overpopulated. Roughly one hundred and ten million people are living on a total land space only half the size of the state of Texas in the Philippines.

At any rate, Dearly and I entered the 'resort' (again, a term being used very loosely here), were locked in by the old woman, and we made our way down to the beach, each of us carrying a backpack. We'd brought only the bare essentials. Food enough for both of us, and booze enough for me, which would have been the equivalent of booze enough for three people, as I was still drinking quite heavily at the time.

We settled into the farthest hut from the main hut on the beach which was obviously used as an office. Though it was now dark, the moon was full, the sky was cloudless and we could see as clearly as if it was day. We enjoyed a late dinner of rice and chicken (it wasn't cold, because it was ninety degrees, but it wasn't nice and hot, either), and then we spent time walking up and down the beach, me carrying a serving tray in one hand with a Filipino candle on it, and my glass of tanduay rum and coke in the other. We had no ice, but the booze had a high alcohol content, so it didn't matter. I was more concerned with effectiveness than pleasantness.

Now, for those of you who don't know what a Filipino candle is, let me explain. You simply take a small jar, or a glass, and you fill it about halfway with sand. Then, you simply pour enough cooking oil into the glass to meet the top of the sand. It will look like mush. Then, you take a toothpick, and you wrap it with a cotton ball by stabbing the toothpick into the ball and then carefully pulling the cotton down over the toothpick, covering it entirely. Next, stick the cotton covered toothpick into the mushy oil soaked sand in the jar, or glass. Wait only a couple of minutes and the oil will entirely soak up and coat all the cotton. You then light the top of the cotton covered toothpick. This is your wick. And it will burn slowly until all the oil from the sand is soaked up through the cotton. This type of candle will actually allow for hours of light.

"I have to pee," I said, after we'd made our way down the beach a way. Our bellies were full, a feeling we'd soon come to forget for a very extended period of time- a time I refer to as my 'down and out years in the Philippines'- and we were going back and forth between wading in the water and walking just where the surf ended against the sand.

"Don't pee there," Dearly warned as I got ready to spray against an old coconut tree stump a few years up from the water's breaking point.

"Why not?" I asked.

"It is the home of the Duende," she said, and I could tell she was serious.

Okay, so the Duende is the magical Filipino dwarf. They are said to live in the jungles, housing in caves they burrow underneath old, coconut tree stumps. This particular stump, where I was about to pee, *did* have a hole in it, but my western, logical mind attributed it to erosion. I laughed and peed on the stump, anyway.

"The Duende," Dearly warned. "He plays many tricks."

I laughed at her, finding her broken English as adorable then as I still do today, after having been with her for eleven years as of this writing, and then I packed my member back into my shorts and turned to walk back to Dearly and return to strolling along the beach, but all of a sudden the Filipino candle that had been resting securely on my serving tray jumped up, flipped in the air, and went crashing to the ground and shattered into pieces. It looked like it happened in slow motion, but in real time I'd been in mid stride and I was unable to stop. When my right foot came down, I sliced the corner of the joint of my big toe, where it meets my foot, clean open on the largest piece of the glass from the candle, and blood began spurting out of my foot like water from a hose.

"Oh, my God!" I shouted. Not only was the injury painful from the slicing from the glass, but the glass was hot from the flame, and it added to the pain. "I'm going to die!"

"Pesti, mata baka!" Dearly said, which is Visayan for 'fuck your eyes.' "I told you the Duende plays tricks. You pee to his house, he cuts to your foot!"

"Fuck my life!" I yelled, a phrase that was pretty common in American pop-culture when I'd left the states. I'd been wanting the opportunity to use it before it died out, like all pop-culture bullshit always does, and thank God for small favors, and this seemed like the perfect opportunity. So perfect, in fact, that I decided to shout it again. "Fuck my life!"

Dearly and I made it back to our hut, me wobbling and her propping me up. Once there, I sat in the bathroom, which was nothing more than a tiled section of the small hut with a hole to defecate and urinate into and a smaller hole under a water spigot which stood as a bathing area. I held a washcloth on my cut and applied pressure, and Dearly left to see if the guard was at the gate. It turned out he was, and both of them returned in just a matter of minutes.

Now, if you have read 'Isle of Kapre' (good on ya, mate, as our English and Australian friends would say), then you'll recognize this scene. When Dearly and the guard came into the hut, they were both carrying the small leaves of the Mulungi tree. I'd eaten these leaves many times in soups and nearly every other Filipino dish I'd ever eaten, but on this night, Dearly and the guard were crushing the leaves up and allowing the juice to drain onto my cut. The instant the juice from the leaves hit my cut, it stopped bleeding, it stopped hurting, and I could almost see it begin to heel. And I would never have the hint of infection as it did hear. It was absolutely amazing. I said these things, and Dearly and the guard both laughed.

"You are Americano?" the guard asked.

"Oh-oh," I said, which means 'yes,' in Visayan.

"In your country," he began, "you take pill for everything. In Philippines, we still use nature. What God gives us."

He had a point.

"In your country," he continued. "You cut foot. You go hospital. You get stitches. You get medicine. You get big bill." He and Dearly both laughed at that. "Here," he said, "you get Mulungi. You go on your way. You keep your money if you have it," he said, and they laughed again.

The guard was at our shack for no more than five minutes. Just long enough to apply ample Mulungi juice to my wound and insult my culture repeatedly. You see, that's one thing about life as a white foreigner in the Philippines. The overwhelming majority of the women love you. They fantasize about you. It's their dream to marry a western man and leave third world poverty behind forever. And anyone who wants to judge them? I would challenge the judge to go without eating for days at a time, and when the judge does eat again, make their meal a chicken neck and a cup of rice, and then go a few more days without eating before repeating the process.

It's not about being whores.

It's about being hungry.

And the men?

Well, many of them, at least, are insanely jealous for aforementioned reasons. Could you imagine being a guy and hearing every female in your life, from your sisters to your mother to the girl you've got a crush on constantly talking about their fantasy of marrying a white foreigner? An entire book could be written on all of this from this point, but... oh yeah.

It was.

It's called 'Isle of Kapre.' Have I mentioned it yet?

Anyway, after the guard left, and I was back on my feet- well, at least one of them- Dearly and I went out and sat on the small front porch of the hut, she eating left over chicken, and me drinking rot-gut Tanduay Rum, now straight, only chasing it with water. Sure, the Mulungi had killed the pain, but I wanted to make sure the Tanduay would perform well as my second stringer in case the Mulungi wore off.

And that's when we smelled it. The smell of sweet cigar smoke. It smelled like the smoke of a cherry flavored Swisher Sweet, something I never saw in the Philippines all the years I was there. .

"It is Kapre," Dearly said, jumping up faster than I've ever seen her move, to this day- well, except the time she stepped on an eight feet long cobra when we were hiking in the jungle, once- and she ran inside and shut the door, leaving me on the porch. "Come inside," I heard her yell from the other side of the door.

"The what?" I said.

Through the door, Dearly reminded me of the Kapre. Sure, I'd heard about it, as well as much of the folklore of the Philippines, but at the time I'd originally heard about it I hadn't taken any of it seriously enough to store it to memory.

And then I heard a twig snap only yards away from the hut, followed by a low growl!

I quickly joined Dearly in the hut, now taking this shit seriously.

Again, and as is fully described in 'Isle of Kapre,' the Kapre is the Filipino version of the North American Bigfoot Sasquatch. However, there are a few stark differences.

Okay, whereas the North American Bigfoot Sasquatch is a forest dweller, the Kapre, who is said to incessantly smoke sweet smelling cigars, lives in the tops of giant trees. Also, he's interdimensional. You see, the Filipino people believe that there is a portal to another dimension in the tops of the trees where this mystical and mythical creature lives, and he uses this portal to go back and forth between our worlds.

Why does he come here? (By the way, Kapres are all males). Well, he comes into our world to kidnap beautiful, young Filipina ladies. He then takes them through the portal and enslaves them as part of his harem on the other side of the portal where he lives in a giant, stately castle.

Think 'Beauty and the Beast.'

Now, in the Kapre's defense, once he gets these young maidens to the other side of the veil, they aren't enslaved by a huge, hairy, hideous beast anymore. You see, the Filipinos believe that once back in his own dimension, the Kapre sheds his hide and alas, he is one hell of a good looking dude.

Anyway, no beautiful, young Filipina lady wants to be taken from her family and her friends on this side of the veil, so it is all so horrifying, and inside our little hut that night, Dearly and I didn't sleep a wink. Oh, we tried, but whatever was on the outside of that hut would not allow it.

"Come on," I said, once in the hut. I'd crawled into bed and got underneath the sheet. In the six years I spent in the Philippines, I never saw a blanket. Hell, they weren't necessary. The temperatures may have dropped to eighty five degrees fahrenheit at night during the two rainy seasons. And you were lucky if you could even find a sheet, but on this night, we were in luck.

"No," she said from somewhere in the hut. She was huddled in a dark corner, as far away from both the door and the one window the hut had as she could get. I looked over at the window, and I saw that Dearly had managed to latch shut the wooden shutters from the inside just before I'd come into the hut, and just as I made the outline of the shutters out in the darkness, they began shaking.

Someone, or some*thing*, was on the outside of the hut, shaking the shudders!

Instantly, I'd forgotten all the jokes I'd made about the Kapre and the Duende and all the other mythical creatures of Philippines folklore. I found myself pulling the sheet up and over my head like a kid watching a scary movie, just like back when I'd watched 'The Exorcist' at four years old, yet this was no movie.

This was real!

Potentially!

Throughout the night Dearly and I would be disturbed, intermittently, by either the shaking of the shutters or the smell of sweet cigar smoke. Every time I'd fall asleep, one or the other, or both, would wake me up, and poor Dearly never even fell asleep at all.

You can only imagine our relief when the sun came up the next morning. You see, just like a vampire, the Kapre will never be seen when the sun is up. It's not that the sun could kill him, he just doesn't want to be seen, so he only comes out, through his portal, under the cover of darkness at night.

When day did come, Dearly and I packed our few belongings. Before leaving his shift, the guard actually came down and helped us carry our stuff up to the gate since he knew my foot was injured. That's one thing I'll give the men of the Philippines. They may be insanely jealous of white foreigners for reasons described earlier, but many of them are still kind, do the right thing and follow the golden rule.

As we made our way past the small hut that was used as an office, Dearly told the old woman of our night. The old woman merely shook her head. She said she didn't sleep all night, knowing something bad was going to happen, and she was just happy that we were still alive. She begged us not to tell of our experience, to anyone, because she was afraid that though the events took place at night, the story might hurt her day business. We promised her we wouldn't tell a soul, but I kept my fingers crossed behind my back, because I knew this story was too good *not* to be told, and now I've told it in two separate books and I've talked about it in several YouTube videos.

But I wish anyone interested in finding this island the best of luck.

It's not even charted on any maps.

My attitude about the Kapre and the Duende and the rest of Philippines folklore changed after that night, and a couple of years and a few 'odd jobs' later, during my 'down and out in the Philippines years,' I would have enough material, by way of actual experience, to pen 'Isle of Kapre,' and to date, it is the most haunting book I've ever written, for you see, though poised as fiction, and though much of it is, I know which parts are not.

I know which parts are real.

And these things, to this day, cost me sleep at night.

Especially since…

…there may be other portals and other large, humanoid cryptids among us…

And there may or may not be one in the woods behind my house on our small homestead here in Virginia.

One that is an entry and exit way for…

…potentially…

Bigfoot Sasquatch!

The End

Lt. Bee Must Die!

(Originally Titled: "The Unfortunate Demise Of Lieutenant Bee)

If you haven't noticed, our stories in this issue of 'Bigfoot Sasquatch Files' are following a particular theme.

Reflection.

It's just occurred to me, over coffee, a blank page, and the sight of two does and one buck eating the few remaining leaves of a peach tree in my fruit orchard just on the other side of the window and down at ground level, as my office is in a second story bedroom, that many of these 'Bigfoot Sasquatch Files' volume focus on themes.

Perhaps it's because I'm in a particular mood when I write them? Perhaps there are issues over which I'm stewing as I type the words?

Well, this is obviously the case, and I'm not too surprised that this issue, Volume 6, written in and released in the month of November, seems to be themed upon the past, for you see, November is the month of my birth, and often, during the month of November, I reflect on my past. It's probably worth noting that November comes toward the end of the calendar year which I'm sure sparks the reflection process in many of us.

So if our last tale was a reflection on the events which inspired my novel 'Isle of Kapre,' I'll take this last tale in our sixth volume to focus on just one of the many stories which inspired much of my novel 'Off Switch;' this work being fresh on my mind as I've recently just made it available in print edition again on Amazon.

There is a particular bad guy in my novel 'Off Switch,' a really shitty lieutenant by the name of Lt. Bee. At least that's what he's called in the book. The book version is a fictional character, but as with most of my works, his character is very tightly based on a real person. It's one of my tricks to the trade, you see. People often ask for advice on writing, and one of my tricks, at least in regard to character development, is that if you tightly base a character on a real person, the work is really already done for you. Is it cheating? Maybe. Is it lazy writing? Maybe. But what I've found is that it's very effective.

Anyway, if you've read the novel "Off Switch" then you know Lt. Bee was a prick. He took great pleasure in abusing and mistreating his troops. Just as it says in the novel, I believe the underlying reason to this day was that he suffered from a severe Napoleonic complex. You see, Lt. Bee was only 5'6" tall. He spent hours in the gym everyday, trying to get buff, which he did, but at most, he put one in the mind of Mighty Mouse, still a somewhat comical sight.

Lt. Bee naturally hated anyone who had what he did not, or at least what he viewed as if he did not have. Things like natural intelligence (he wasn't stupid), or alpha-male strength, speed and/or natural leadership qualities. He worked hard to obtain these things, and that's commendable, but I honestly believe he always viewed himself as lesserthan because he hadn't been born with or naturally gifted with these attributes. And I'm sure it didn't help him in our unit that our first sergeant was pure alpha-male stud! An airborne infantryman who stood six feet six inches tall, weighed a solid two hundred and twenty pounds, and who had women melting whenever he passed because of his movie star and manly rugged, good looks.

And then here came Lt. Bee, nearly jogging, having to take almost three strides to keep up with the first sergeant's one.

Here is a fact about our deployment that Lt. Bee was completely unaware of while we were in Mosul, Iraq fighting for our lives, the freedom of the Iraqi people, and, despite what so many of my neighbors in my very 'enlightened' community of Charlottesville, Virginia (a University town), tell me- the sheer survival of Western Civilization, as the factions we faced in Iraq were desperately trying to reunite with other factions in the region to deliver a death blow to Western Civilization. Here is a fact I thought I'd take to my grave. Yes, this fact that Lt. Bee never knew of while he was abusing many of his troops, treating us as if we were his enemy, because we'd been gifted with what he lacked.

People were trying to kill him.

Not the terrorists.

His troops.

Here is a cold hard fact of war that most folks who've never been to war do not know. Even those who served in the military but who never deployed do not know this.

There's nothing friendly about friendly fire.

It's intentional.

So much so, that in the recent wars in the Middle East the Defense Department actually changed the term 'friendly fire' to 'fratricide,' meaning 'to kill my brother.'

Why?

Because even those at the Defense Department knew that what had been called friendly fire for centuries was not friendly, but intentional.

So, here's the deal. I had no idea, until after we'd left Iraq and were de-mobing in Ft. McCoy, Wisconsin, just how many of my fellow troops had it out for Lt. Bee. You see, despite being surrounded by your fellow soldiers, enemies, explosions and gunfire while in a combat zone, your brain turns so much of what is around you off. It has to in order to maintain any semblance of a brain. In order to avoid going completely and unrecognizably insane. Nothing about war makes sense, and nothing that takes place in a combat zone is logical. But one does what one must do in order to survive, and after the insanities pile up so deep, the brain simply shuts down.

So, here is a list of things that were going on around me in regard to the close demise of Lt. Bee while in Iraq, things of which I had no idea, because I was walking around with combat induced tunnel vision (if anyone or anything steps within my life of sight, I either kill it or I don't kill it. It's that simple).

1- Sgt. T- whom Lt. Bee hated with a passion, because Sgt. T's father was a command sergeant major with another unit (by the way, that's the highest rank one can achieve in the enlisted ranks), cut the brake cables one night, toward the end of our deployment, of the uparmored humvee that Lt. Bee would be riding in that night. Sgt. T would be driving, and his plan was to simply go out in a blaze of glory, over a cliff with a two hundred feet drop in a particularly mountainous region of northern Iraq that we crossed through every night while out on convoy, taking, of course, Lt. Bee out with him.

What stopped Sgt. T's plan? At the last minute, they switched out his machine gunner. Sgt. T didn't particularly care for his regular gunner. He didn't hate him, but he had no problem with considering him collateral damage in Lt. Bee's demise, but he was rather fond of the gunner with which he had been switched. His new gunner was a young private whose mother Sgt. T had personally promised he would make sure came home. So, while in the motor pool, preparing to go on mission that night, Sgt. T declared the guntruck inoperable due to a problem with the brakes, and the truck was switched out for another.

Lt. Bee would live to abuse his troops another day.

2- Specialist C was the gunner on the truck that roamed our convoy for side security. Specialist C's truck was positioned in the middle of the convoy, and if any of our gun trucks had issues and needed to stop for any reason, it was Specialist C's truck's duty to hurry up and pull side security, while another truck hurried into place on the other side of the stopped truck, and yet another rushed to pull rear security (this, by the way, was my truck). This way, any stopped truck in our convoy always had full, three hundred and sixty degree security, and each gunner only had to secure a forty five degree piece of the line of fire pie.

One of of SOP's (standard operating procedures) was that we were *never* to dismount (that means get out of) our gun trucks, because the most effective weapon our enemies were using against us was IED's (improvised explosive devices). They knew they could not fight us, and win, toe to toe. They knew their weaponry was far inferior to ours (we could shoot them dead from ranges their weapons could not even reach us from), so they would bury bombs along the roadsides and try to lure us into their detonation zones and blow us up. It was much safer to be inside those uparmored vehicles in case an IED exploded than it was to be outside them.

Lt. Bee fancied himself a cowboy. Anytime we stopped for any reason, he would jump out of his truck and strut around with his M-4 assault rifle drawn, like he was going to kill every damn terrorist in the Middle East all by himself. And what he didn't know was that by eighty percent of the way through the deployment, every time he got out of the gun truck to strut around with his assault rifle, Specialist C, from high atop his turret in the gun truck parked alongside Lt. Bee's, had the sights of his fifty caliber machine gun trained on the back of Lt. Bee's head.

His plan?

Should a firefight go down?

Specialist C was going to take Lt. Bee's top knot (that would be his head, for you civilians reading this), off with his fifty caliber machine gun and write it all up to 'friendly fire.' He knew he'd be taking a risk now that the term used was 'fratricide,' but it was a risk he was willing to take.

Now, at this point, you may find yourself feeling sorry for Lt. Bee. You might be asking yourself what it was that he was doing that would lead so many among our unit to think of ways to kill him?

I won't prolong this point, because many of the things he was doing were clearly pointed out in 'Off Switch,' but what I'll tell you, is that at the time of his abuses, many of us feared his abuses would have very long lasting effects on those of us he was abusing, and now, more than ten years after the abuses were dealt out by way of Lt. Bee, I can tell you that we were right.

To this day, I have three adult children who were innocent little kids while their Daddy was in Iraq fighting monsters, and being abused by a monster who wore the same uniform as Daddy, who I have not seen or heard from in nearly a decade, and the beginning rift in this sad relationship split was a direct result of Lt. Bee's abusive actions toward me in Iraq (that whole taking me off the payroll and not allowing me to go to the payroll department and get put back on- hence- having no ability to send money home to my family while deployed, setting it up perfectly for my ex-wife to take my kids and go anywhere she pleased with them ((she picked England, of all places)), and not giving me a say, because I was a 'deadbeat dad' anyway, and yes, there are soldiers who fight in combat zones without pay, while their families suffer back home, you just never hear about it... because those stories don't work as tear jerker space fillers in mainstream media like the ones they use where Daddy comes home from deployment and surprises his daughter who is out cheering at the local high school football game).

I must stop at this point, because the previous sentence (which looks more like a paragraph) that I just wrote is completely incoherent. I've intentionally not edited it, because some things cannot be edited. They must not be, for it takes away the true feeling and meaning. Let's consider that last sentence (that looks like a paragraph) a practice in what's called point of conscious writing.

The point is.

I still suffer from the effects of Lt. Bee's abuses more than a decade after the fact.

And I didn't even mention his disallowing of me to seek medical treatment when I was injured for the entire remaining three months of our deployment, which would lead to a six month Army hospital stay with surgery and rehab and the onset of painkiller addiction, ending what had previously been eight years of being clean and sober before that, and...

Here we go again.

The point is (seriously, this time).

Lt. Bee had to die.

But he didn't.

Yet...

***

As I mentioned, I learned of all these plots against the life of Lt. Bee only after returning to the U.S. from Iraq. I've mentioned only two, but there were many, many more (and I'd be lying not to admit that I had a few of my own). The most haunting, however, was the plot that was described in the least detail.

Danny's plot.

Danny and I had been CHU (company housing unit) mates in Iraq with a couple of other guys. That means roommates. The four of us shared a plywood box twenty feet by twenty feet for nearly a year. It was like a sweatbox. There was enough room for all our gear, and then we'd somehow manage to find a place to lay within our gear and sleep for four hours or so when we were on base.

Oh, and the whole sweatbox reference? It's because our air conditioner was always going out, and Lt. Bee wouldn't allow us to go to the maintenance guys who fixed such things and report it. One of us would always sneak, and then the officer in charge of repairs would ride up one side of Lt. Bee's ass and down the other for abusing his troops, and then Lt. Bee would ride up one side of our asses and down the other, like taking us off the payroll, etc. for having gotten our air conditioner fixed and him in trouble while doing so.

Danny didn't talk much, but when he did, what he said was profound. He was a computer whizz, knew more about world history than any professor I ever had in college, read more books than anyone I ever knew (including me, and at times I read ten books a month), and in a word, was just an all around genius.

And he'd never finished high school.

Danny didn't look it, but physically, he was formidable. He looked kind of 'doughy,' which as you know, is a state that precedes fat. Yet he could run mile after endless mile and nearly keep up with me, and I have an extensive track and field background. He wasn't buff, and he didn't look strong, but he could lift far more weight than me. And though he moved slowly and methodically, and had a babyface, on the combatives mat (that means MMA mat for any civilians reading this), he would choke out our most skilled fighters.

Oh, and he was obsessed with Bigfoot Sasquatch.

It didn't come to any surprise for me, at the time, because we were in Washington State, and many of the guys in our unit were obsessed with Bigfoot Sasquatch. Well, we were in Ft. McCoy, Wisconsin, but my unit was with the Washington Army National Guard, so you get my drift.

What the hell was I doing in Washington State?

I'd moved to Washtington from Virginia, because my ex wife had moved to Seattle, in order to try to get my kids away from me (as far as possible, obviously), and max out child support payments, due to that whole number of nights at each parent's house thing. Too bad for her, when she moved, leaving the kids with me for six month so she could get set up in Seattle, all unannounced to us, she lost custody and I was awarded full custody, and she was supposed to pay child support (which she never did, but of which I never cared, because I just wanted my kids). I'd sent the kids to stay with her while I did my military training then took the high road and moved out to Washington once I was finished so that our kids could have their mother *and* their father in their lives. It was never about money. It was about the kids.

And three months later I was in Iraq with the Washington Army National Guard.

And I've already told you the rest.

"He's going to die," Danny said. Again, we were at Ft. McCoy when this conversation took place. We'd just finished our little pow-wow. The one where all the guys who'd been planning on killing Lt. Bee in Iraq but who never did had left. Only Danny and I remained in the room. "He's going to die in six or eight years. No one from our unit will be suspected."

"What are you talking about?" I asked Danny, knowing him well enough to know that the words he spoke were not empty. There was meaning to them. I knew that Danny had a plan.

"I know where he lives," Danny said. "I know where he hunts."

Lt. Bee was one of those psychos who'd joined the Army to kill people, not to defend his county. And for anyone wondering, there *is* a difference. Lt. Bee hunted to kill animals, not for food, though he did eat what he killed, but again, he hunted for the sheer joy of killing.

In his free time Lt Bee watched a DVD series called "Prison Fights," an illegal blackmarket film series where prison guards would set up fights in prisons and sell the DVDs for profit. One of the rules in "Prison Fights" which drew Lt. Bee's sick mind to the series was that once you knocked out or choked out your opponent, you did *not* have to stop fighting. Fighters could and often would continue to beat the man they'd knocked out, often to death. These were the fights that Lt. Bee watched over and over while we were in Iraq.

"I've seen shit in those woods," Danny continued, "and that shit is empathic, and he's going to get a little too close to what I've seen, and they're going to know exactly what he's thinking and why he's out there, and…"

"This isn't more of your Bigfoot Sasquatch bullshit, is it, Danny?" I said.

"Lake," he said, sounding irritated, but he really wasn't. Not by now. He had been at first, but we knew each other well now. "It's either Bigfoot, or it's Sasquatch. It's not both."

"It's all make believe," I said, so it can be whatever I want it to be."

"Let's go to chow," Danny said, and we did.

***

So, I guess you were hoping for a more detailed, lengthy conversation between Danny and me, about what sort of unfortunate demise Lt. Bee would end up having? I wish I could give you one, but that's all there was to it. Like Mark Twain said, fiction is harder to write than non-fiction, because fiction has to at least make sense. Well, here's his case in point. This short, simple, almost nothing burger conversation between Danny and me about Lt. Bee's future death, at the hands of a Bigfoot Sasquatch nonetheless, seems hardly worth writing about, right?

Wrong!

While reminiscing a few days ago, because it is November and all, November, of course, being the month of my birth and the tail end of the calendar year, I decided to look up my old friend Danny. Unfortunately, and as with all the guys I deployed with, I'd lost touch. I'd spend six months in the Army hospital after our deployment, and then I lived in the Philippines for the better part of six years, and I was fighting for my life as much over there in many different (yet a couple similar) ways as I had been in Iraq, and staying in touch with best good buddies just wasn't on the top of my priority list at the time, and now I'm settled in Virginia, and, well, people just lose touch is what I'm getting at in this near incoherent paragraph of a sentence.

I Googled him, and I found out that Danny was dead.

Danny had died by way of a single vehicular accident on an old state route just outside of the small timber town in Washington State in which he'd been born and raised. The only times he'd left that small town was to go to a rock concert (Linkin Park) in Seattle, basic training in Ft. Sill, Oklahoma, and to defend his country and all western civilization in a little shithole of a city known as Mosul, Iraq.

He was thirty years old at the time of his death.

I shed a tear for my old friend, though I wasted no energy on the emotion of guilt for having been out of touch. Shame and guilt are the two most worthless emotions we can spend energy on, and it took me nearly forty years to learn this, and I refuse to unlearn it. It is what it is.

Though it is unfortunate.

And Lt. Bee?

Well, of course I had to Google that son-of-a-whore after shedding a tear for Danny.

He's dead, too.

I wish I could say that he'd died at the hands of Bigfoot Sasqutch, but he did not.

Since our unit was a national guard unit, the guys in the unit *did* have day jobs when not deployed and not training one weekend a month and two weeks a year during summer annual training.

Lt. Bee was a computer programer, and, as it turned out, after getting home from Iraq he landed a job working with computers for none other than the Washington State Department of Corrections.

He was programming computers in prisons!

About a year after Danny's deadly car accident, Lt. Bee, by then *Major* Bee, as his illustrious actions in Iraq had earned him a promotion, was found dead in a library in one of Washington's many state prisons. He'd been beaten to death, it's assumed by an inmate, though it's never been determined who the inmate who'd allegedly beaten him to death was. No one's talking, because as even those of us who've never been to prison know, in prison, snitches get stitches, bitches!

No motive of the deadly beating was ever revealed. And investigators, to this day, have never been able to figure out why Lt. Bee's body (again, Major Bee at the time of death) was found, lying on the floor of the library, with a camcorder lying on one side of his body and a crisp, one hundred dollar bill on the other.

Personally, I have reason to believe I know what Lt. Bee had been up to just before his unfortunate demise. I have reason to believe that he propositioned the wrong inmate to star in one of his warped videos he'd planned on selling on the black market, and he got his just deserts.

But what do I know?

I'm just some batshit crazy war vet now obsessed with Bigfoot Sasquatch himself.

Like my old friend, Danny.

God rest his soul.

The End

Made in the USA
Middletown, DE
02 December 2020